DUMP TRUCK

BULLDOZER

GHOSTER GRADER

MONSTER-VATER

FRONT LOADER

ROLLER MASHER

BACKHOE

FIEND GRUBBER

CRUSHER MUSHER

CEMENT MIXER

CRANE

MONS
ON MACH

DIRTY DUGG

GORBERT

HARCOURT, INC.   Orlando Austin New York San Diego London
Printed in Singapore

TERS
INES

DEB LUND

Illustrated by

ROBERT NEUBECKER

STINKY
STUBB

MELVINA

Construction crew monsters arrive on the scene.
They don hard hats before they go near a machine.

Leather work gloves,
some earplugs,
and big, heavy boots
are required for safety
by all builder brutes.

Stinky Stubb's the mechanic. He checks out the grader, the tractor, the cranes, and the big monster-vater.

Once engines are greased and the gears start to spin,
he shrieks to the others that work can begin.

Foreman Gorbert stomps over. He's huge and he's hairy.
He grunts out the orders and adds, "Make it scary!"

The site's almost ready. The blueprints are drawn.
It's a Custom Prehaunted with thistles for lawn.

Dirty Dugg mounts the backhoe. He's tough as a troll.

He can dig, dump, deliver, and leave a big hole.

Vile Melvina's front loader attacks all the muck.
First she pushes and packs it, then calls in a truck.

Flinging dirt like tornadoes, they holler and hoot.

(Monsters love getting grimy from hard hat to boot.)

They're transformed by the tractor, the crawler, the paver.
But bulldozers bring out *true* monster behavior.

They take turns on the steamroller, forklift, and crane,
till construction and cleanup are all that remain.

The cement trucks arrive. The foundation is poured.
Then they carefully place every brick, every board.

When the building is up and they gaze at the sight,

they can hardly contain their disgusting delight.

"How enchanting!" "How spooky!" "How frightfully fine!"

"The colors all clash. The design is divine!"

Then an eerie dark shadow eclipses the sun.

Their hearts begin racing.

They're ready to run.

Their stomachs all churn—

what's she bringing today?

Might a slimy concoction be heading their way?

She takes out a cloth and then spreads it just so,
placing napkins and plates in a neat little row.

From her basket she pulls out a black iron pot.
It smells really good—like it's starting to rot.

"Mama, tell us what's in there!" they cry. "Pretty please?"
"It's your favorite," she says. "Monsteroni and cheese!

Remember your manners. Sit up, now, and eat."
So they shovel it in with their hands and their feet.

When they finish with lunch, they crawl up on her lap,
and she reads them a story before they all nap.

Soon enough they'll be toiling
until the job's done,
but for now they're on blankies,
worn out from the fun.

With a stretch and a yawn, they awake from a dream.
After Mama gets hugs, once again they're a team.
Stinky Stubb checks the engines. Dugg's ready to dig.
Foreman Gorbert tells Mel to get back on her rig.

Once the landscaping, sidewalks, and roads are complete,
it's time to clean up so all's tidy and neat.

Without too much whining, they each do their share.

Melvina, Stubb, Gorbert, and Dugg know what's fair.

So clear out of the way if you see them around—
they're an organized earthquake reshaping the ground.
These builders are proud of the job that they do...

...on their mud-mounding,

nail-pounding,

monsterous crew.

For our own little
monster, Jean Michael
—D. L.

For my beasties,
Izzy and Jo
—R. N.

Requests for permission to make copies of any
part of the work should be submitted online at
www.harcourt.com/contact or mailed to the following
address: Permissions Department, Harcourt, Inc.,
6277 Sea Harbor Drive, Orlando, Florida 32887-6777.
www.HarcourtBooks.com

Library of Congress Cataloging-in-Publication Data
Lund, Deb.
Monsters on machines/Deb Lund;
illustrated by Robert Neubecker.
p. cm.
Summary: Construction crew monsters arrive on the
scene with tractors, cranes, and grader machines, and
after a gruesome site is created as their routine, they
straighten it up and leave everything clean.
[1. Monsters—Fiction. 2. Construction workers—Fiction.
3. Construction equipment—Fiction. 4. Stories in rhyme.]
I. Neubecker, Robert, ill. II. Title.
PZ8.3.L9715Mo 2008
[E]—dc22 2006037393
ISBN 978-0-15-205365-9

First edition
H G F E D C B A

Printed in Singapore

The illustrations in this book were done with India ink
on watercolor paper and then colored digitally.
The display type was created by Robert Neubecker.
The text type was set in Farmer.
Color separations by Chroma Graphics (Overseas)
Pte. Ltd., Singapore
Printed and bound by Tien Wah Press, Singapore
Production supervision by Christine Witnik
Designed by April Ward

CEMENT MIXER

GOOBER SCOOPER

FIEND GRUBBER

GHOSTER GRADER

CRUSHER MUSHER

BACKHOE

ROLLER MASHER

74

CRANE

BULLDOZER

MONSTER-VATER

FRONT LOADER

DUMP TRUCK

For Dad—and the snows of yesteryear—FSC

For Terry—SS

The morning sky was steely **gray**,
and hungry as two bears
we sniffed downstairs but couldn't find
our breakfast anywhere.

Maple Syr
the best M

Mom said, "Get dressed, my little cubs.
Pull on your **brown** snowsuits.
Grab your scarves and hats and gloves.
Zip up those new snow boots."

"We're going to the farm," Dad said.
"You want to know the reason?
To hunt for winter's hidden gold—
It's maple syrup season!"

Some neighbors and school friends were there.
We had a snowball fight,
then rode a sleigh that made **blue** tracks
through fields of glittering white.

A snowman pointed out the way,
and what do you suppose?
A plump **red** cardinal landed on
his **orange** carrot nose!

2 miles

We passed a yellow tractor chuffing
puffs into the freeze

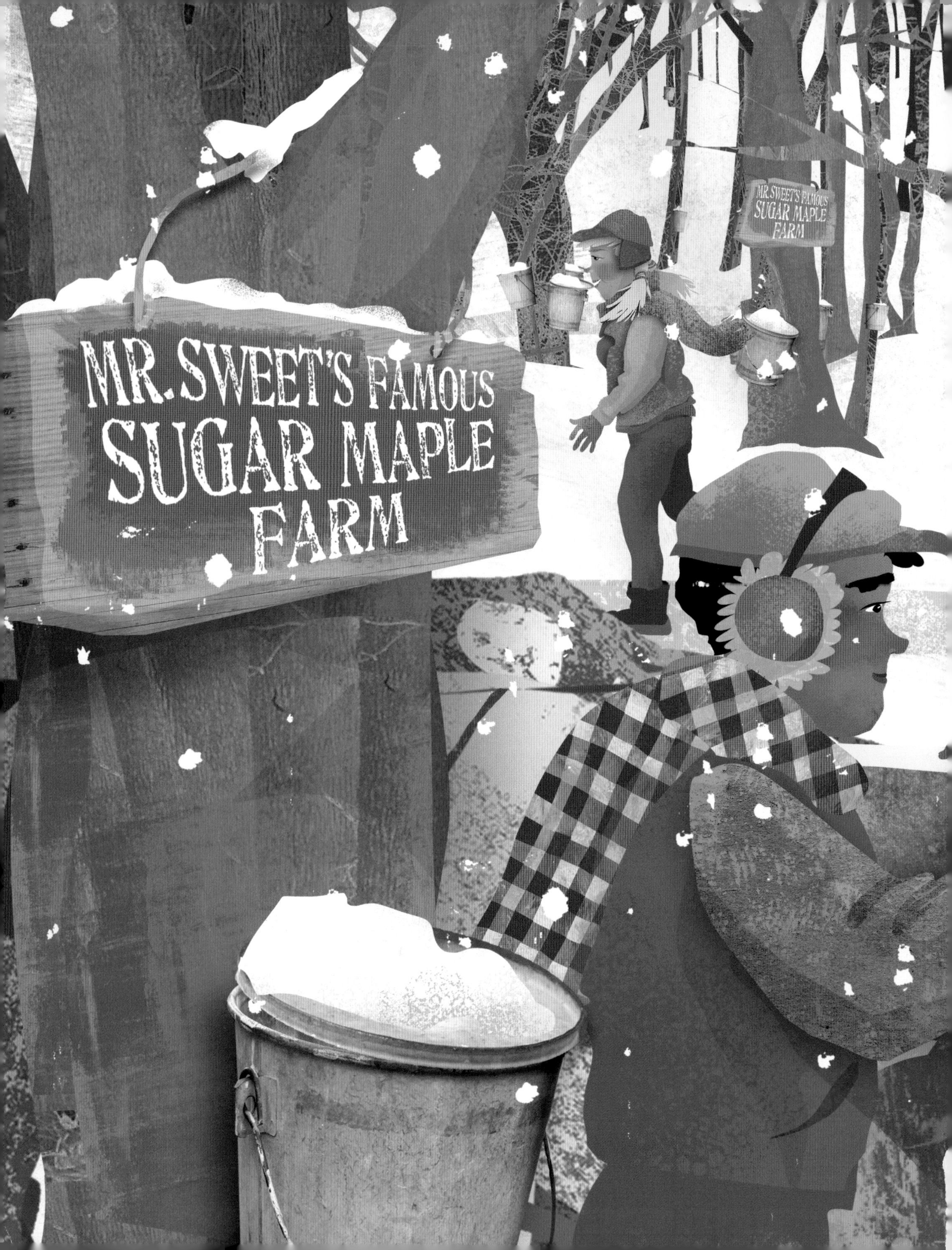

and stopped with bright **pink** cheeks aglow
beside some maple trees.

Each tree contained a wooden tap.
A **silver** pail below
collected all the clear, sweet sap.
The farmer said, "Let's go!"

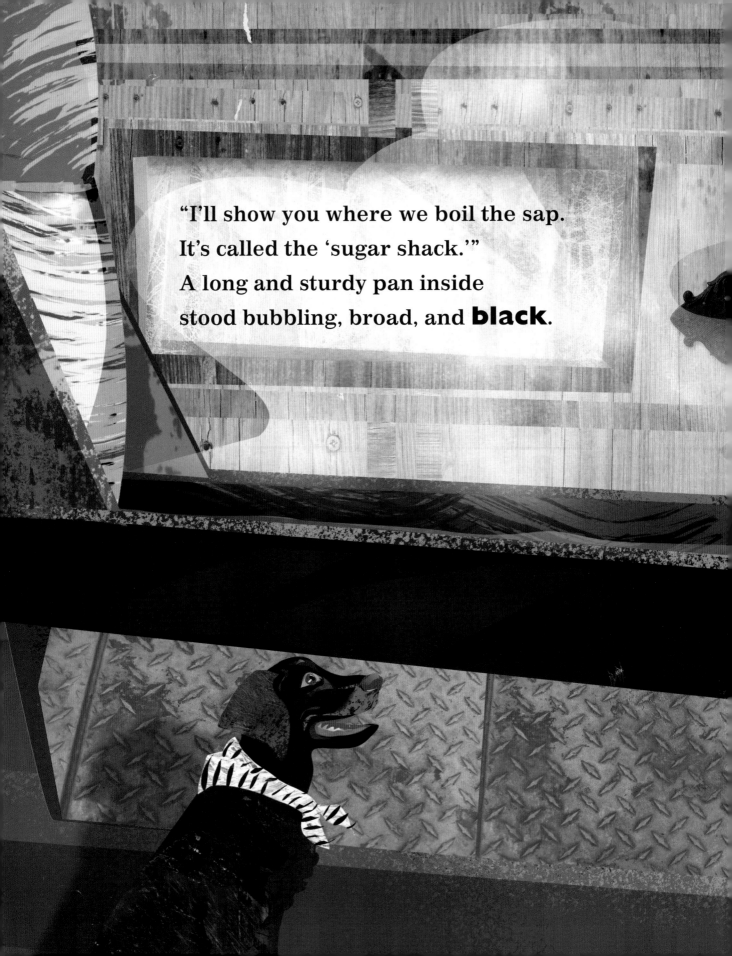

"I'll show you where we boil the sap.
It's called the 'sugar shack.'"
A long and sturdy pan inside
stood bubbling, broad, and **black**.

The **amber** syrup smelled so good
it made our tummies growl.
We hadn't had our breakfast yet
and went out on the prowl.

We rode down hills of **purple** shadows

through rows of **evergreen**.
The farmhouse was the sweetest sight
that we had ever seen!

And while a winter **rainbow** bloomed
on farmhouse coatrack pegs,
we warmed ourselves on pancake smiles
with syrup, hash, and eggs.

Our tummies full, we bundled up
to brave the cold, crisp air
and traveled on—white sun on snow,
bright colors everywhere!

Also by Felicia Sanzari Chernesky and Susan Swan:

Cheers for a Dozen Ears:
A Summer Crop of Counting

Pick a Circle, Gather Squares:
A Fall Harvest of Shapes

Library of Congress Cataloging-in-Publication Data is on file with the publisher.

Text copyright © 2014 by Felicia Sanzari Chernesky
Illustrations copyright © 2014 by Susan Swan
Published in 2014 by Albert Whitman & Company
ISBN 978-0-8075-7234-4
Printed in China
10 9 8 7 6 5 4 3 2 1 BP 18 17 16 15 14

The design is by Nick Tiemersma.

For more information about Albert Whitman & Company,
visit our web site at www.albertwhitman.com.